Ready Steady Read!

Dear Parents,

Congratulations! Your child has embarked on an exciting journey – they're learning to read! As a parent, you can be there to support and cheer them along as they take their first steps.

At school, children are taught how to decode words and arrange these building blocks of language into sentences and wonderful stories.

At home, parents play a vital part in reinforcing these new-found skills. You can help your child practise their reading by providing well-written, engaging stories, which you can enjoy together.

This series – **Ready, Steady, Read!** – offers exactly that, and more. These stories support inexperienced readers by:

- gradually introducing new vocabulary
- using repetition to consolidate learning
- gradually increasing sentence length and word count
- providing texts that boost a young reader's confidence.

As each book is completed, engaging activities encourage young readers to look back at the story, while a Picture Dictionary reinforces new vocabulary. Enjoyment is the key – and reading together can be great fun for both parent and child!

Prue Goodwin
Lecturer in Literacy and Children's Book

D0271230

1

How to use this series

The **Ready, Steady, Read!** series has 4 levels.
The facing page shows what you can expect to find
in the books at each level.

As your child's confidence grows, they can progress
to books from the higher levels. These will keep them
engaged and encourage new reading skills.

The levels are only meant as guides; together, you and
your child can pick the book that will be just right.

Here are some handy tips for helping children who are
ready for reading!

Give them choice – Letting children pick a book
(from the level that's right for them) makes them
feel involved.

Talk about it – Discussing the story and the
pictures helps children engage with the book.

Read it again – Repetition of favourite stories
reinforces learning.

Cheer them on! – Praise and encouragement
builds a child's confidence and the belief in their
growing ability.

LEVEL 1 For first readers

* short, straightforward sentences
* basic, fun vocabulary
* simple, easy-to-follow stories of up to 100 words
* large print and easy-to-read design

LEVEL 2 For developing readers

* longer sentences
* simple vocabulary, introducing new words
* longer stories of up to 200 words
* bold design, to capture readers' interest

LEVEL 3 For more confident readers

* longer sentences with varied structure
* wider vocabulary
* high-interest stories of up to 300 words
* smaller print for experienced readers

LEVEL 4 For able readers

* longer sentences with complex structure
* rich, exciting vocabulary
* complex stories of up to 400 words
* emphasis on text more than illustrations

Make Reading Fun!

Once you have read the story, you will find some amazing activities at the back of the book! There are Excellent Exercises for you to complete, plus a super Picture Dictionary.

But first it is time for the story . . .

Ready?

Steady?

Let's read!

Ragnhild Scamell   Gaby Hansen

The Wish Cat

LITTLE TIGER PRESS
London

Holly's house had a cat
flap. But Holly did not
have a cat.

One night, Holly saw a
falling star.
"I wish I had a
kitten," she whispered.
Suddenly . . .

CRASH!

Something landed outside. But
it was not a kitten. It was Tom
– the scruffiest cat Holly had
ever seen.

"But I wished
     for a kitten,"
          cried Holly.

Holly hid under
     her quilt.

The next morning,
Tom brought Holly
a smelly fish.

"Yuk!"
said Holly.

And she shooed
him away.

But Tom just sat
on the swing . . .

and washed his
coat noisily.

At lunchtime, Holly gave
Tom a bit of her sandwich.

In the afternoon, Tom
followed Holly around . . .

chasing leaves...

balancing on
the fence . . .

showing off.

"Bye then, Tom," said
Holly, stroking his head.

Tom settled himself on
the doorstep.

That evening,
it snowed.
Tom curled up
to keep warm.

Holly ran to the cat
flap and held it open . . .

"Poor old Tom," she said.

And she dried him with
the kitchen towel.

Holly stroked Tom's scruffy fur. Suddenly, another star fell. Holly could not think of anything to wish for. She had everything she wanted. And so had Tom.

Excellent Exercises

Have you read the story? Well done!
Now it is time for more fun!

Here are some questions about the story. Ask an adult to listen to your answers, and help if you get stuck.

Wonderful Wish

In this story, Holly wishes for a kitten. If *you* could have any wish, what would it be?

Bits and Bobs

Can you name some of the objects in this picture? What kind of things do you have outside *your* front door?

Tom Cat

Now describe what Tom is doing in this picture.

Warm and Cosy

Can you remember how Holly gets Tom warm at the end of the story? How do *you* keep warm when it is cold?

Picture Dictionary

Can you read all of these words from the story?

Holly

house

night

leaves

quilt

sandwich

shooed

snowed

Tom

towel

Can you think of any other words that describe these pictures – for example, what colours can you see? Why not try to spell some of these words? Ask an adult to help!

Hopping Mad!

Fred has five frogs. Finn has five frogs, too. And when ten frogs get together, it is party time! But Fred and Finn do not find the froggy madness very funny . . .

Newton

Newton keeps hearing funny noises! "Don't be scared!" he tells his toys. And he sets off in the dark to find out what is making the scary sounds.

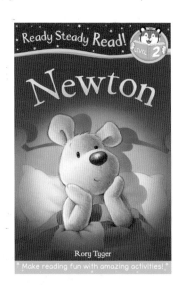

Ouch!

Hedgehog is about to go to sleep when OUCH! an apple lands on her back! Will her friends be able to help her?

Where There's a Bear, There's Trouble!

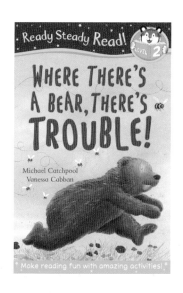

Where there's a bee there's honey. So when Bear spies a bee, he chases after it. But, where there's a bear, there's trouble. So the bee buzzes off as fast as it can ... !

To Thomas James, with love – R S
For Mum and Dad – G H

LITTLE TIGER PRESS, 1 The Coda Centre, 189 Munster Road, London SW6 6AW
First published in Great Britain 2001
This edition published 2013
Text copyright © Ragnhild Scamell 2001, 2013
Illustrations copyright © Gaby Hansen 2001, 2013
All rights reserved
Printed in China
978-1-84895-676-6
LTP/1800/0589/0413
2 4 6 8 10 9 7 5 3 1

Books in the Series

LEVEL 1 - For first readers

Can't You Sleep, Dotty?

Fred

My Turn!

Rosie's Special Surprise

What Bear Likes Best!

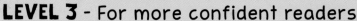

LEVEL 2 - For developing readers

Hopping Mad!

Newton

Ouch!

Where There's a Bear, There's Trouble!

The Wish Cat

LEVEL 3 - For more confident readers

Lazy Ozzie

Little Mouse and the Big Red Apple

Nobody Laughs at a Lion!

Ridiculous!

Who's Been Eating My Porridge?

LEVEL 4 - For able readers

The Biggest Baddest Wolf

Meggie Moon

Mouse, Mole and the Falling Star

The Nutty Nut Chase

Robot Dog